Foot-Foot's Feats

Foot-Foot Meets Riff-Raff

This Book Belongs To:

_____

Some bunny loves you.

"Nanny... can you tell me a Foot-Foot story?" Well Kaylin... yes, Nanny can, and will every year. Nanny shares these stories with you, your sister Sophie, and cousins Reed and Elle, so they can always be a special little part of your lives.

...

Kaylin - you inspire me.

Once upon a time, there were three little bunnies

named Foot, Foot-Foot, and Foot-Foot-Foot.

One day, on their way home from school, they saw their friend Roxy kneeling on the sidewalk. She was picking up her belongings from her knapsack. The boys could tell she had been crying and noticed her knapsack was ripped.

"Hi Roxy. What happened?" asked Foot-Foot.

"There's these three boys who are really mean to me," explained Roxy. "They're always calling me names, and today they ripped my knapsack. Look, my stuff's all over the ground."

The three brothers looked at each other and realized they had a serious situation unfolding. At the same time they all said, "We will help you, Roxy." So they went over to Roxy, helped her up, then helped her put her goodies back in her knapsack.

While they were gathering up Roxy's goodies, Roxy began to explain that there were three other Bunnies that were bullying her: Hang-Nail, Toe-Tag, and Riff-Raff. Every day they would wait for her after school and shout bad names at her. Normally they did not touch her, but today, they crossed the line!

Foot, being the oldest and wisest of the three brothers, felt they had to get more information in order to determine why this was happening. After all, Hang-Nail, Toe-Tag, and Riff-Raff didn't bully anyone else. Or did they? Hmmmm...

"Why do you think they are bullying you, Roxy?" Foot asked.

"I think it's because they think I am different," she said.

"Why would they think that?"

"Well," Roxy started, "one day Toe-Tag walked me home, took one look at our house, then at me, and stormed away."

"What made him do that?" Foot-Foot-Foot asked.

"I'm not entirely sure," she said, "but you're welcome to come to my house and see if you can figure it out."

"Okay," they said, then off they went to Roxy's house.

It turned out Roxy's home was bright, colorful, and well, definitely different! But the Foot-Foot brothers thought this was fun and exciting.

"Can we see what it looks like on the inside?" asked Foot-Foot.

"I'll have to ask Mummy and Daddy first. Oh, and thank you for walking me home," Roxy replied.

The boys said, "You're welcome, and we'll see you in the morning."

That night at the supper table, the boys explained to their Mummy and Daddy what was happening to Roxy. Mummy's response was, "That's horrible. I'm sure Roxy is lovely, and I'm so proud of you boys for helping her." Then Daddy said something about "holding their feet to the fire" and "someone going toe-to-toe" with them.

Foot, Foot-Foot, and Foot-Foot-Foot looked at each other, confused, then asked Daddy what he meant.

So he explained, "Where it is within your ability to help someone who needs help, you need to do it. It's a big ole world out there, boys, and we need to be kind to each other and accepting of our differences."

Mummy looked at Daddy then said, "Remember when we were in high school and you had to get braces for your teeth?"

"Yes," Daddy said, "I had quite the overbite."

She continued, "There were a few kids that made fun of Daddy's braces, and sometimes they could be very mean to him. Most days Daddy would try to avoid them or just plain run away from them. He hoped they would stop on their own."

"Did they?" asked Foot-Foot.

"No," Daddy said. "I was scared and intimidated. I thought if I told anyone I would get in more trouble with the bullies. Then, one day I was hiding in the school cloak room, waiting for the bullies to leave, when my teacher asked me what I was waiting for. I took a big breath and told her my situation. It felt so good to tell someone. She held my hand and said 'Let's go make a couple of phone calls.'"

"Who did she call, Daddy?" asked Foot.

"The principal, my mother, and father, and the bullies' parents – we all had a meeting about the situation and made a plan to resolve our issues."

"Did it work?" Foot-Foot-Foot asked.

"Yes, son, it did. So, I would encourage you to tell Roxy to speak to her parents."

A lightbulb came on over all three bunnies' heads, and they had the same idea. When they walked to school with Roxy tomorrow, they would tell her to let her parents know about Hang-Nail, Toe-Tag, and Riff-Raff. In the meantime, they wouldn't let Roxy out of their sight.

The next morning, they arrived at Roxy's to find her mother and father getting ready for a parade and putting Roxy's sister in her car seat. "Have a good day at school Roxy! We love you, and don't forget to take your medication!"

Meanwhile, Roxy's sister Nadine said "Wuv oo Woxy." Nadine was only two, so sometimes her words came out differently. Roxy said bye to her family and joined Foot, Foot-Foot, and Foot-Foot-Foot on their walk to school.

Halfway to school, just as they came to a very wooded area, Hang-Nail, Toe-Tag, and Riff-Raff jumped out in front of them.

"Who do we have here?" asked Riff-Raff. "More weirdos like you?"

Roxy looked at all three of them and said "N-n-n-no. These are my friends."

"Yeah, right." said Toe-Tag. "Who would be friends with the likes of you?"

"Likes of her?! It's more like the other way around," challenged Foot-Foot.

"Huh?" the bullies said. "What are you talking about?"

Foot-Foot stepped forward and said, "Roxy is kind, smart, and fun. You'd have to be a complete moron to not recognize that."

Well, Hang-Nail, Toe-Tag, and Riff-Raff thought they were a lot of things, but "moron" was not one of them.

Hang-Nail put his shoulders back, hopped over to Foot-Foot, looked him straight in the eyes, and stated, "Is that right, Smarty-Pants! I think you're the one that's a moron!"

Before Foot-Foot could say anything, they heard a super loud sound.

Roxy had put her fingers to her lips and produced the loudest whistle they had ever heard. Birds flew out of the trees, gophers popped their heads out of their holes, and everyone except Roxy had eyes as wide as saucers.

"Holey Free-holey!" the bullies exclaimed.

"Yeah... what they said!" said the Foot-Foot Brothers.

"How do you know how to do that?" Hang-Nail asked.

"My daddy taught me how, so that if I ever needed to get attention or wanted to make noise at a football game, I could do it with this type of whistle," explained Roxy.

"I've never heard anything like it OR as loud. What a great way to get attention," said Hang-Nail. Riff-Raff and Toe-Tag nodded in agreement.

"Would you show us how to do it?" asked Hang-Nail.

"Unexpected" was the first thought Roxy had. She looked at Foot, Foot-Foot, and Foot-Foot-Foot, scratched her ear and then said, "Leave it with me. All three of you have been so unkind and hurtful to me. Right now it's hard for me to imagine doing something nice for you."

Riff-Raff, Toe-Tag, and Hang-Nail looked at her sheepishly. They knew she was right, and they felt sorry for how they had treated her. They really wanted to know how to do that whistle. It was so cool.

That night at the supper table, Roxy opened up to her parents. She told them all about the bullying and the situation she now found herself in.

"Why should I be nice to them when they've been so mean to me? I just want them to go away and leave me alone."

"Sweetheart," Daddy explained, "when people don't understand or feel threatened by someone or something, they often make fun of it in order to make themselves feel better about themselves. My nanny once told me, 'Two wrongs don't make a right.'"

"What did she mean by that?"

"It means, just because someone is behaving badly or doing mean things, that doesn't give you permission to do the same. If so, you would be no better than them."

"Oh," said Roxy. "Well... I don't think I could show them how to do the whistle thing. Could you?"

"I think that's a great idea! Your mother and I will reach out to their parents and make arrangements."

And so the planning began.

Foot, Foot-Foot, and Foot-Foot-Foot even got invited to the Whistle Workshop. Everyone showed up at Roxy's house at 9 am sharp that following Saturday. Their home was vibrant, fun, and inviting. There were caramelized carrots (of which Foot-Foot-Foot ate four), stuffed cabbage leaves, and yummy carrot juice for everyone.

Daddy was patient and kind while he instructed and demonstrated how to do the two-finger whistle. At first there were a lot of whooshing sounds, but it wasn't long before the whole crew were whistling so loud that Daddy said, "It's time to move this party outdoors!"

Foot, Foot-Foot, Foot-Foot-Foot, Hang-Nail, Toe-Tag, Riff-Raff, and Roxy were all so focused on the whistling that they forgot they had differences. All they were aware of is what they now had in common… the two-finger whistle!!!

Just then, Foot-Foot had a glorious idea.

"Let's form a club!" Foot-Foot said. "A Whistler's Club. We can go to sporting events, parades, and parties and really liven everything up. Maybe we can even learn to whistle music and be like a Whistle Choir."

Well, you would have thought Foot-Foot had given them all a million carrots, because their eyes lit up, their ears stood straight up, and they started hopping around everywhere. "I'll take that as a yes," he said, and Roxy gave him a big bunny hug and thanked him.

Roxy's daddy gathered everyone together and told them how proud he was of them. He said something about "putting your best foot forward" and "reaping what you sow" – which was okay with them, even if they weren't really sure what it meant.

After the Whistle Workshop, the Bunnies forgot about any differences they had. Hang-Nail, Toe-Tag, and Riff-Raff each apologized to her for being so mean and promised never to bully her or anyone else, and they meant it. After all, they felt happy and really did like Roxy.

"You're cool, Roxy," said Foot.

"You three are pretty cool too," Toe-Tag said. "All this time we've been mean and ugly..." He shook his head. "We missed out on knowing some great people and having terrific times."

"And all it took was a whistle," said Foot-Foot.

That night, Foot dreamed of being a football referee for the NFL. Foot-Foot dreamed of being a police officer directing traffic, and Foot-Foot-Foot dreamed of being at a concert and cheering them on with his crowd pleasing whistles.

Life is but a dream.
Row your own boat.

The End

Printed in Poland
by Amazon Fulfillment
Poland Sp. z o.o., Wrocław

58548173R00026